DELIGHTFUL KEY CLASSICS

The Three Bears

Retold by Jane Carruth

Illustrated by Gwen Tourret

RAMBORO

Once upon a time there was a little girl with golden curls called Goldilocks, and there were Three Bears who lived in a wood and who didn't know anything about the little girl until one day . . . Well, on this particular day Goldilocks got up very early and went into the woods. And the Three Bears got up very early and went down to breakfast.

Now there was a great big enormous Bear – he was Father Bear. And there was a plump middle-sized Bear – she was Mother Bear. And there was a wee tiny Bear – he was Baby Bear.

The Three Bears always ate porridge for their breakfast. Father Bear's porridge was always in a great big enormous bowl and he had a great big enormous spoon to eat it with. Mother Bear's porridge was always in a pretty middle-sized bowl and she had a middle-sized spoon to eat it with. And Baby Bear's porridge was always in a wee tiny bowl and he had a wee tiny spoon to eat it with.

When the porridge was ready Mother Bear always went to the foot of the stairs and called up, "Father Bear, your porridge is all ready and on the table. Baby Bear, come down at once. Your porridge is on the table."

And Father Bear and Baby Bear would tumble down the stairs into the neat tidy kitchen of their cottage and sit down at the table.

Father Bear sat in a great big enormous chair. Mother Bear sat in a comfortable middle-sized chair and Baby Bear sat in a wee tiny chair.

On this particular morning when Father Bear tasted his porridge he cried, "The porridge is far too hot to eat right away!"

"So it is," squeaked Baby Bear, as he tasted his porridge.

"Then we must let it cool," said Mother Bear sensibly. "We can all go out into the woods and enjoy the fresh air."

So the Three Bears went out into the woods for a walk and they didn't lock the door of their cottage because they did not expect any strangers to visit them so early in the morning.

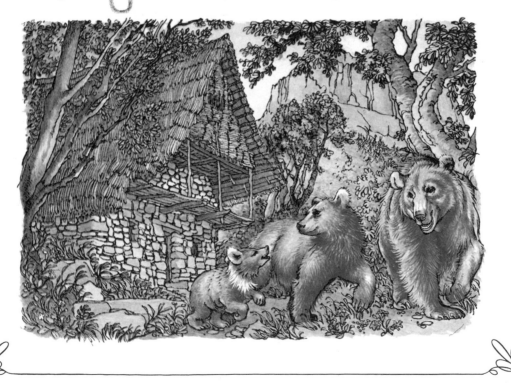

They had only been gone for a short while when along came Goldilocks. She had been running about in the woods for quite a time and she was tired and hungry. When she saw the cottage she ran up to the front door and knocked. But no one came, so she went round to one of the windows and peeped into the kitchen. It was empty.

"I might as well go inside," Goldilocks told herself. "There is nobody to stop me!"

So she pushed open the cottage door and went inside. She was so hungry that the smell of the delicious creamy porridge tickled her nose and she ran straight into the kitchen.

There on the table sat three bowls of lovely porridge.

There was a great big enormous bowl, a pretty middle-sized bowl and a wee tiny bowl. Goldilocks, being a greedy child, went to the great big enormous bowl and tasted the porridge it held.

But, oh dear me, the porridge in the great big enormous bowl was so hot that it burnt her tongue and she dropped the spoon and turned quickly to the pretty middle-sized bowl.

But, oh dear me, the porridge in the pretty middle-sized bowl was so cold that she made a face and dropped the spoon. Then she went to the wee tiny bowl. The porridge in the wee tiny bowl was neither too hot nor too cold and Goldilocks liked it so much that she ate it all up.

"That was very good," said Goldilocks, licking her lips. "I wish there was more of it."

And she took the wee tiny spoon and scraped the bowl just to make sure that there wasn't even the tiniest bit of porridge left in it. Then she yawned and rubbed her eyes for now she was beginning to feel ever so tired and sleepy.

She looked around the neat tidy kitchen but she could not see any comfortable chairs to sit in. So she left the kitchen and went into the living room.

Now you will be thinking that Goldilocks was a naughty girl, for you know perfectly well that it is not very nice to eat someone else's porridge and to make yourself at home in someone else's house.

But Goldilocks was a naughty girl so she did not feel at all sorry that she had eaten up all the porridge or that she meant to sit down in one of the three chairs she saw in the living room.

One was a very big enormous chair and you can guess, can't you, who sat in that chair! The second was a pretty middle-sized chair, and you can guess, can't you, who sat in that chair! The third was a wee tiny chair and you can guess, quite easily can't you, who sat in that chair!

Goldilocks went first to the very big enormous chair and flopped down into it.

But, oh dear me, the chair was much too hard for her and she frowned and jumped out of it quickly. Then she went to the middle-sized chair and sat down in that.

But, oh dear me, that chair was much too soft for her and she threw its pretty cushion on the floor and moved across to the wee tiny chair, which was Baby Bear's very own special chair, and she sat down in that.

Baby Bear's chair wasn't too hard, and it wasn't too soft. In fact, it was just right. It was the sweetest, dearest little chair Goldilocks had ever sat in, and she smiled as she wriggled about in it to make herself comfortable.

Then she thought that it might be fun to bounce about in the little chair, and so she bounced up and down – not once but three or four times – until, oh dear, suddenly the bottom fell out, and two of the chair's slim legs broke, and Goldilocks found herself sitting on the floor!

"Stupid, silly old chair!" Goldilocks exclaimed, picking herself up. "Why did you have to break?"

And she wasn't a bit sad that she had broken the dear little chair. She was only sorry that she couldn't sit in it any more. Well, there wasn't another chair in the   living room   except, of course, the two she had already sat in. So she went upstairs to the bedroom.

The Three Bears had a very pretty bedroom. There were bright curtains on the windows and honeysuckle paper on the walls and a fresh green carpet on the floor, the colour of grass. There was certainly nothing in the bedroom to make Goldilocks think that it belonged to three bears!

If there had been something to make her suspect who owned the room she might not have decided to stay there for very long! For little girls don't often get on very well with bears. But there was nothing.

Father Bear's bed was nearest to the door. It was a great big enormous bed with a big heavy pillow.

Next to it was Mother Bear's middle-sized bed, with its cosy pink eiderdown and pink frilly pillows.

Baby Bear's bed was a wee tiny bed. It stood close to the window and it had a bright blue cover on it and a bright blue pillow-case on the pillow. No wonder Baby Bear was so proud of his wee tiny bed! And no wonder he slept so soundly in it every night.!

But Goldilocks liked the very big enormous bed and decided that it would suit her very well so she flung herself down on it, knocking the pillow on to the floor.

But, oh dear me, the bed was much too high at the head for her. It didn't suit her at all, and she didn't stay in it for very long. With an impatient sigh she jumped out of it, and went to the middle-sized bed which stood beside it.

Its pretty pink eiderdown slipped on to the floor as she scrambled into the bed, but Goldilocks did not trouble to pull it up for she knew almost as soon as she got into it that the middle-sized bed was not for her. It was much too low at the foot.

"Bother!" she exclaimed in a bad-tempered way. "I won't sleep a wink if I stay in this horrible bed. It is much too uncomfortable for little girls like me!"

And she jumped out and went over to the wee tiny bed which stood close to the open window. And she looked at it for a minute, and she thought about it, and she decided that at last she had found a bed that would suit her very nicely.

Well, the wee tiny bed wasn't too high at the head for her. And it wasn't too low at the foot for her. It was just exactly right!

Goldilocks bounced up and down on it once or twice just to make quite certain that this was the bed for her.

Then she put her head on the blue frilly pillow, and she snuggled down under the blankets, pulling the sheet right up to her nose.

After her big breakfast of porridge and her long search for a nice place to rest she felt very, very tired.

Soon she had closed her eyes and was fast asleep.

Meanwhile, as she slept, the Three Bears were beginning to think about their breakfast.

"I'm hungry," squeaked wee tiny Baby Bear.

"I'm hungry too," said very big enormous Father Bear.

"Then let's go home at once," said middle-sized Mother Bear. "Our porridge will be cool enough by now."

When the Three Bears reached their cottage they went straight into the kitchen to eat their breakfast.

The first thing Father Bear noticed was the porridge which Goldilocks had left on his spoon, and he growled in a very big enormous voice,

"Somebody has been eating my porridge!"

Mother Bear looked at her porridge and she too saw that there was some porridge sticking to her spoon. So she cried in her middle-sized voice,

"Somebody has been eating my porridge!"

Then Baby Bear saw that he didn't have any porridge left in his bowl at all, and he squeaked in his wee tiny voice,

"Somebody has been eating my porridge and has eaten it all up!"

Now the Three Bears were very cross, and Father Bear led the way to the living room to find out if their uninvited visitor was there. When he saw that his big enormous chair had been pushed to one side, he growled in his great big enormous voice,

"Somebody has been sitting in my chair!"

Mother Bear looked at her middle-sized chair, and when she saw that its cushion was on the floor, she said in her middle-sized voice,

"Somebody has been sitting on my chair!"

Then suddenly Baby Bear squeaked in his wee tiny voice,

"Somebody has been sitting in my chair – and has broken it all up!"

And he rubbed his eyes and began to cry, for he loved his wee tiny chair.

The Three Bears were now very cross indeed.

"We'll go upstairs and see if there is anyone is our bedroom," said Father Bear.

So the Three Bears stumped upstairs to their bedroom. As soon as they were inside they stopped beside Father Bear's very big enormous bed which, as you know, was nearest to the door. The heavy pillow was lying on the floor, and Father Bear said in his very big enormous voice,

"Somebody has been lying in my bed!"

Then they all went over to Mother Bear's middle-sized bed. Its pretty pink eiderdown had slipped to the foot of the bed and was touching the floor and when Mother Bear saw this, she cried in her middle-sized voice,

"Somebody has been lying in my bed!"

Now it was time for the wee tiny Bear to go over to his bed. The eiderdown was in its right place and so too was the pillow. But on the pillow was a little girl's golden curly head. And the wee tiny Bear knew that it had no business to be there – no business at all.

"Somebody has been lying in my bed – and here she is!" Baby Bear squeaked in his wee tiny voice.

The very big enormous Bear and the middle-sized Bear went over at once to Baby Bear's wee tiny bed.

They stared down at the sleeping Goldilocks as if they could not believe their eyes. Then they stared at each other, and Father Bear scratched his head with one of his big enormous paws. And Mother Bear shook her head from side to side. They could not understand how such a pretty girl came to be asleep in Baby Bear's bed.

And still Goldilocks slept on. She had not heard the very big enormous voice of Father Bear. She had not heard the middle-sized voice of Mother Bear. She had not even heard the wee tiny voice of Baby Bear who had spoken so close to her ear.

But then suddenly Baby Bear let out a shrill high squeaky squeal. And Goldilocks did hear that! At first she thought it was part of her dream. But then she knew that it wasn't when she opened her eyes and saw the Three Bears!

Would you be frightened if you woke up to find three bears looking down on you? You might be – especially if one of the bears was a very big enormous one!

Goldilocks was so frightened that she rolled over and fell out of bed. She landed on the floor with a thud. But she didn't give the Three Bears enough time to ask her why she had entered their house, and eaten their porridge, and broken the wee tiny chair and slept in the wee tiny bed.

Oh no! Before you could say *crackle-snap*, she had scrambled to her feet and was making her escape.

Well, there wasn't anywhere she could go except through the open window, and so that was the way she went. It was lucky for her, wasn't it, that the window wasn't very high up, and that she landed on a soft carpet of grass!

"She's running away!" squeaked Baby Bear. "Stop her!"

"She's reached the garden gate already," said Father Bear, going to the window. "Now she's disappearing into the woods."

"We won't ever see her again," said Mother Bear, going to her bed and pulling the pretty pink eiderdown right. "I'm sure we won't."

"I suppose not," said Baby Bear. "But she had very bright curls, didn't she?"

And he smoothed his sheets and punched his blue pillow until it was nice and fat again.

Then Father Bear said he was hungry, and Baby Bear said that he was very hungry too, for they had walked a long way through the woods. Mother Bear said it was all the fault of the naughty girl with the golden hair that they had missed their breakfast, and now it was cold.

So the Three Bears went downstairs to the kitchen, and Mother Bear straight away began making fresh porridge. And Baby Bear, because he was so pleased to smell the lovely porridge, began washing the bowls and the spoons, and putting them back on the table ready for their breakfast again.

And while they were busy, Father Bear went off to the tool shed for his tools and soon he had mended Baby Bear's wee tiny chair. He mended it so well and so carefully that it looked just as good as new by the time he had finished, and nobody would ever have guessed that not long before a little girl had sat in it and broken it all up! Then he picked up all his tools and carried them back to the shed.

When the porridge was cooked Mother Bear made sure that it wasn't too hot and it wasn't too cold. In fact it was just exactly right! So she ladled it into the three bowls that Baby Bear had set out on the table, and the Three Bears ate up every bit of it. Baby Bear even licked his wee tiny spoon until it shone like a silver penny, and there wasn't the tiniest scrap of porridge left.

Then Father Bear went into the living room and sat down in his great enormous chair and fell asleep. And Mother Bear settled herself in her middle-sized chair with its pretty cushion and she too fell fast asleep.

As for Baby Bear – he was so happy to find his wee tiny chair mended as good as new that he sat down in it at once instead of going out to play. And there he stayed for a long time, and he thought about the strange little girl with the golden curls who had eaten his porridge and sat in his chair and slept in his bed – and, yes, just for a teeny weeny moment, he wished she would come back so that he could find out her name.

But, of course, Goldilocks never did go back to that cottage in the woods, and the Three Bears never saw her again!